MOMMY ALWAYS COMES BACK

WRITTEN AND ILLUSTRATED BY:
KRYSTAL CARTER

Library of Congress Control Number: 2023919078

ISBN-13: 979-8-9892908-0-2

Dedicated to:

My lovely daughter
Aubreigh. Your life
inspires me!

Tomorrow is the day I dread. Mommy said,
"The first day of school lies ahead."

I even explained how I never want us to be apart, but she said school is going to make me bright and smart.

Mommy tucked me into bed
so tight. I slowly drifted off
feeling sad and slight.

Morning came, and mommy
kissed my cheek.

I held her
tight, feeling
small and
weak.

With a heavy heart, we reached the car. My tummy churned, emotions bizzare.

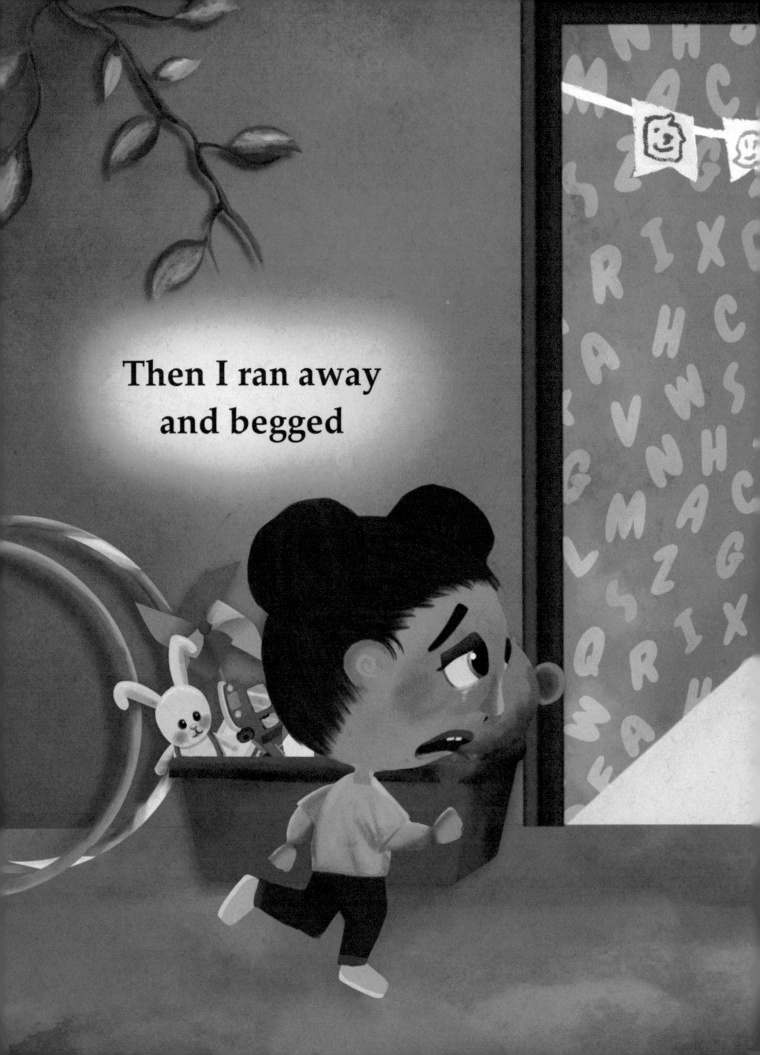

Then I ran away
and begged

"MOMMY PLEASE DONT GO!"

Mommy got down on one knee
and softly whispered to me,
"Just remember, mommy will
always come back."

A friendly boy named Dan took my hand. He said, " Don't be afraid, this is where the fun begins !"

We ran to the playground and slid down the slide.

I even saw a big blue bike I could ride !

We ate
snacks.

We played
games.

We even
sang
songs!

But soon nap time came and I realized my mommy was gone.

I sadly hugged
my teddy and
laid in my
sleep sack.

Then I remembered
and whispered to
myself, mommy
said she will always
come back.

I smiled and felt better as I drifted away.

I woke up to my teacher yelling, "It's time to play!"

I ran to the rug to play with the toys.

I played with my new friends while feeling such joy.

Suddenly, I heard the door open and who did I see?

It was my mommy's smiling face looking at me!

My new friend
walked into the room
and said, "Wow look
at that!"

My mommy picked
me up and said see?
I'll always come
back!

THE END

About the Author

Krystal Carter is not just an illustrator; she's a multi-talented creative force, an author, entrepreneur, and a devoted mother. Hailing from the sunny state of California, Krystal's journey as an artist is a testament to her self-taught spirit and boundless imagination. Krystal's love for art was ignited during her childhood, and with each passing year, her passion only grew stronger.

One of Krystal's greatest joys is sharing her artistic vision with the world and inspiring others to embrace their own unique talents. Her dedication to helping others be the best version of themselves shines through her work, whether it's bringing stories to life as an illustrator, crafting captivating book covers, designing delightful coloring books, or immortalizing moments in breathtaking portraits.

Krystal has become a cherished collaborator for fellow authors, elevating their stories with her artistry. Her artistic endeavors know no bounds, and she's constantly exploring new avenues to express her creativity and touch the lives of those who encounter her work.

Krystal is a creative soul who continues to leave her mark on the world through her remarkable illustrations and boundless imagination.

MOMMY ALWAYS COMES BACK

Made in United States
Troutdale, OR
01/18/2024

17003599R00026